For my friend Paula Danziger

First Edition

Library of Congress Cataloging-in-Publication Data

Brown, Marc Tolon.
    Arthur's TV trouble / Marc Brown. — 1st ed.
      p.   cm.
    Summary: When Arthur sees advertisements for the amazing doggy
Treat Timer, he decides to earn enough money to buy it for his dog,
Pal.
    ISBN 0-316-10919-3
    [1. Advertising—Fiction.   2. Money-making projects—Fiction.
3. Brothers and sisters—Fiction.   4. Aardvark—Fiction.]
I. Title.
PZ7.B81618Aoke   1995   94-48816
[E]—dc20

10 9 8 7 6 5 4 3 2 1

WOR

Published simultaneously in Canada by
Little, Brown & Company (Canada) Limited

Printed in the United States of America

It all started while Arthur was watching *The Bionic Bunny Show*.

"Dogs love 'em," said the announcer. "The amazing Treat Timer. Treat your pet to Treat Timer. Only $19.95. Treats may vary. Batteries not included. If you love your pet—get a Treat Timer!"

"Wow!" said Arthur. "Pal needs one of those."

Ads for the Treat Timer were everywhere.

Now Arthur really wanted one.

Arthur counted his money. D.W. helped.
"Even with all my birthday money," he said, "I only have ten
dollars and three cents."
"I know what you're thinking," said D.W.
She ran to protect her cash register.

Arthur decided to ask Dad for an advance on his allowance.
"Gee, I'd love to help," said Dad, "but my catering business is
a little slow right now."

Arthur knew Mom would understand.

"Money doesn't grow on trees," said Mother, "and I think Pal likes treats from you, not a machine."

On the way to school, Arthur was walking very slowly.
"What are you doing?" asked Buster.

"Looking for money," said Arthur. "I want to buy Pal a Treat Timer."

"Those are very expensive," said Buster. "You need a job."

"I need a miracle," said Arthur.

At school, while everyone else took the spelling test, Arthur daydreamed about the Treat Timer. Mr. Ratburn asked Arthur to stay after school to take the test over.

Arthur took the long way home so he could think of a good excuse for why he was late. Mr. Sipple was cleaning his garage.

"Hi, Arthur," he said. "Every fifty years I clean the place out.
I could use a little help."
"I could use a little money," said Arthur.

"All these newspapers need to be recycled," said Mr. Sipple. "I'll pay you fifty cents a stack to take them out to the curb."

"Great!" said Arthur. "I'll do it tomorrow."

"I won't be home until after dinner," said Mr. Sipple, "but you can get started. Everything you need to do the job is here."

"I'm rich!" thought Arthur.
All of a sudden, Arthur was in a big hurry to get home.

"I've got a job!" cried Arthur. "Now I can buy a Treat Timer!"
"Can I go to the mall with you?" asked D.W.
"Sure," said Arthur.
"I wish you were rich all the time," said D.W. "You're much nicer."

The next day, Arthur counted the stacks as he pulled them to the curb. Twenty-four.

"That makes twelve whole dollars!" cried Arthur. "I'll come back later to collect!"

"You look exhausted," said D.W. when Arthur got home.
"I don't want to see another newspaper for a long, long time,"
said Arthur.

"Well, then don't look out the window," said D.W.

"So that's what the string was for!" said Arthur. "I'd better hurry before Mr. Sipple gets home."

"Wait for me," said D.W.

"You're in big trouble," said D.W.

"You missed some over there.

These stacks could be a lot neater.

Are you using double knots?"

"Nice work!" said Mr. Sipple when he got home. "Here's your twelve dollars."

"Thank you, sir," said Arthur.

"I helped," said D.W. "Don't I get something?"

"You get a trip to the mall, remember?" said Arthur.

The next morning, Arthur and his family were the first ones at the mall. Arthur put his money on the counter. "One Treat Timer, please," he said.

"It looks bigger on TV," said Arthur when he saw the box.

"You assemble it, of course," said the salesperson. "And remember, all sales are final."

Five hours later, the Treat Timer was assembled.
"You're going to love it, Pal," said Arthur.
Pal sniffed it.
Arthur turned it on. It clicked. Lights flashed.

Treats shot out like rockets.
Pal let out a loud bark and ran for cover.
"Turn it off!" yelled Mother.

"I'm trying to," said Arthur. "But I think it's broken."
"And remember," said D.W., "all sales are final."
Arthur went to his room to be alone.

"I'm worried," said Mother. "He's been up there for hours."
"I know how to get him out," said D.W.
"It's seven o'clock," she yelled up the stairs. "*The Bionic Bunny Show* is on!"

Seconds later, Arthur appeared.

"Sit down," said D.W., "so I can protect you from those nasty commercials."

"I don't need these!" said Arthur. "There's no way a TV ad will get all my hard-earned money again."

"It's the Magic Disappearing Box!" said the announcer. "Astound your friends! Eliminate your enemies! The Magic Disappearing Box from KidTricks!"

"Hmmm," said Arthur. "Now, this could be useful."

"What would you ever do with that?" asked D.W.

"Oh," said Arthur. "You might be surprised."